Tombstone Bustin'

FRANCES FORBES HEYN

Tombstone Bustin'

Illustrations by

JEAN CHARLOT

Stratford Press   Athens, Georgia

© 2000 by Frances Forbes Heyn
Illustrations © Frances Forbes Heyn
and the estate of Jean Charlot.
Originally written in 1978.

Published by Stratford Press
Athens, Georgia 30605
All rights reserved

ISBN 0-9671886-1-X

Printed in the United States of America
by Maple-Vail Book Group

Songs reproduced in this text
were taught to the author by Bessie Jones
and can also be found in *Step It Down*
by Bessie Jones, published by
the University of Georgia Press.

Contents

Foreword

Walter Stephens

My first memories of Frances stretch back to summer and then winter days and evenings of the late 1940s and '50s. Between her journeys to places mysterious to a nine or ten year old, she visited our rural south Georgia home. This lady, tall and thin, crowned with straight, dark, shiny hair, and with skin bronzed to an indian color, produced from her suitcase treasures that were exotic and exactly right for a boy who, at that time, had been no further afield than the boundaries of his home county.

Once it was the skin of a small mountain lion; once a foul-smelling jar of something called "grasa del tigre" (grease from a jaguar); once a decorated scabbard for a machete. She would stay sometimes a week—sometimes part of a season, and then be off to new discoveries.

The central area in our house was a large living room that boasted a large, open fireplace at one end, a Steinway at the other. During late afternoons in the winter, after the fireplace had struggled against northwesterly winds all day, to prevent freezeup, Frances would uncover the piano keyboard and run scales, then chords.

She usually started with a few songs which appealed to a young boy but she always ended with her special interpretation of "Indian Love Call." In listening and watching, it seemed as though the song were being more than merely sung, but performed by one who, herself was an indian—wise with the knowledge of wild rivers and secret magical places. Not only did her resonating voice fill the room with humanity, but her enthusiasm and smiling personality provided a warm coating for winter evenings.

It seemed as though she had always been "almost" a part of our family. Perhaps indeed she had been: she and my father became friends while students at the University of Georgia. After college, the friendship expanded to include my mom and continued until the deaths of my parents.

Throughout her life, Frances has been closely connected to the intellectual and art community both in Georgia and abroad. The connection was genetic as well as environmental. She was born in Athens on the University of Georgia campus. Her aunt, Lucy M. Stanton, was an internationally acclaimed artist who remains known for miniatures as well as oils. One of her brothers, W. Stanton Forbes, who was on the faculty of the University, was an author as well as an artist.

Frances received her B.S. and M.S. degrees and an Art Education Certificate from the University of Georgia. During 1928–29, she received a fellowship to study preschool education at the Merrill-Palmer Institute in Detroit. For 13 summers she organized and directed Camp Chatuge, a girls' camp in the north Georgia mountains.

During the early 1940s she married Lt. Roswell Drake Ison. After his death, she served in the Red Cross at the Army General Hospital near Tuscaloosa.

Her teaching background included directorship of the nursery school at the University of North Carolina Women's College; child art education in the Charlotte, North Carolina city schools; various preschool and elementary programs for the University of Georgia and the Athens city schools. She was acting director of the University of Southern Mississippi Division of Home Economics Nursery School.

In 1950, she married Anton J. Heyn, a scientist and professor at LSU. After moving to New Orleans, she joined the staff of the "Over 50 People's Program" and taught yoga exercises for 20 years.

In 1941, Lamar Dodd, head of the University of Georgia Art School, invited the internationally acclaimed muralist, Jean Charlot, to become artist in residence. During this tenure, Frances was in charge of preschool education for two of the Charlot children.

Then began an enduring friendship with the artist and his wife, Zomah. At one point, after Frances shared an early version of the manuscript "Tombstone Bustin'," the artist used blue and brown colored pencils to sketch drawings describing key story points.

It was spring or early summer when I first heard the story. Frances—or rather, "Aunt Frances"—and I were in the back yard of our rural home. I was eight or nine. I remember the warm sun, the tall pines; I remember her expressive, mellow voice drifting over the dialect and her eyes becoming wide when Old Emma Jones took Little Job's bandanna.

The story is about voodoo; a belief and practice in the supernatural brought to America on slave ships. From today's lofty level of knowledge, we probably consider such beliefs rather primitive and unsophisticated, but to rural south Georgia Blacks during the first half of the 1900s, hexes or curses easily caused young wives to run away and the healthy to die. Usually the only way to remove the curse was to contact a voodoo doctor. You paid him and he said the right words—maybe even mixed a potient.

But, thin our modern veneer of enlightenment with a little common sense and maybe we understand that belief in voodoo was neither primitive nor extinct: most folks today attend church and pray for good fortune and good health. Then, in order to ensure favorable answers to these prayers, they contribute funds for buildings or add coins to the collection plates.

Frances' manuscript and Charlot's drawings have rested too long in unopened files. It is time they were enjoyed by those who have an interest in a good story about decent people: a story that took place during a time that was before television; before air conditioning; before computers— a time when people were bound closer to the earth, a time that was fond, less complex—maybe better—a time that is no more.

A good story written by one who is more than "almost" family—a life long friend.

January 2000

Frances Forbes Heyn met Jean Charlot when he was artist-in-residence at the University of Georgia from 1941 until 1944. During this period, he painted two murals on campus, one on the exterior of the Fine Arts Building and another in the College of Business Administration (then the Journalism Department), and taught numerous students.

In the 1970s, an exhibition catalog for the Georgia Museum of Art said this about Charlot:

Born in 1898 in Paris where he received his early education, Charlot immigrated to Mexico in 1921 and enrolled at the Coyoacan Art School where he came to know many of the artists later associated with the Mexican Mural Movement. In Mexico City, he painted a mural in the National Preparatory School which, according to his own account, was the first true fresco produced in the New World in modern times.

Jean Charlot was a cosmopolitan figure in American art. Born into a family of international connections, he was educated in France and served for a period in the French Army of Occupation after World War I. While still in his mid-twenties, he was a key figure associated with Diego Rivera in the crucial early days of the Mexican Mural Renaissance. From the 1930s through the 1960s, he was artist-in-residence at many leading art schools. . . . It was during this period he was associated with the University of Georgia.

In 1945, the University of Georgia Press published a book of *Charlot Murals in Georgia*. Following his stay in Georgia, Charlot received a Guggenheim Fellowship to write the book *Mexican Mural Renaissance*, subsequently published by Yale University Press.

Tombstone Bustin'

Old Neptune's Daughter

Joseph awakened from a dream of fire and noise coming out of the elements. Bessie declared it a sign of trouble revealed to him. This disturbed her for Joseph had been born with a veil over his face and so, like her and his great-grandfather, had a gift of prophecy and ability to see and to talk with spirits. Except for this, Joseph and his twin brother were exactly alike; both had shiny black skins, deep saltwater eyes, and study square bodies.

After hearing Joseph's dream, Bessie was reluctant to turn them loose to their own devices, but she did, for today was cleaning day. What took place later when Job lost his red bandanna they dared not confess, but it was to weave into their

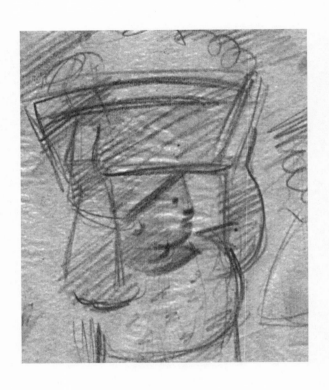

lives a scarlet patch of color they could never forget.

As usual, when free, Job and Joseph chose to explore some part of the Island. They decided to go down the oyster-shell road and up the sand path to an old graveyard, because Joseph felt unusually close to spirits. The faint path the boys followed led to an eerie spot in the deep wild, only shafts of light penetrated the lavish spreading mass of unsorted vines and leaves overhead, trailing moss moved ghost shapes in the breeze. Job saw Joseph nod his head and say, "Howdy."

"Who that you say howdy to, Joseph?" whispered Job, seeing nothing.

"That was a spirit," explained Joseph.

"Well, what did he say?" asked Job.

"He said, where you goin'?"

"Why didn't you tell him, Joseph?" asked Job.

"Well, he knew. Anyway he wasn't expecting no answer except 'howdy,'" replied Joseph.

"What did he look like, Brother Joseph?" asked Job.

"Oh, he looked like just a man," Joseph's tossed-off answer irritated Job.

They wandered on now, each lost in his own feelings of spring. Spring had come again to the island which lay quiet in the sun off the coast of Georgia, cut from the mainland by a flat, salt river and long stretches of green marshland. The beaches on the other three sides spread fan-shaped splashed by sea brightness. All winter these two boys watched for the first signs of spring, peepers singing loudly from the marshes at dusk, for the edges of the marshes to turn green, blue swamp lilies and wild phlox to crowd the roadways and cover the dunes by the sea. They came upon Liza and Essy gathering wild pink honeysuckle and wood violets which they crowded into huge baskets carried on their heads to the village to sell. Rollicking along behind them came Bee, the blackest and most beautiful of them all, with a flame camellia in her hair, filling the lane with her laughter. All these spring things the boys were aware of, but most of all the warm, rich black earth, the hot sand beneath their feet, and the comfort in their bones.

They had reached the crumbling wall which surrounded the small old cemetery plot. The

woods stood still, no bird sang to disturb those in quiet sleep, snowdrops and daffodils pushed their silent way through the brush to border the graves, reminiscent of black-veiled ladies who stopped to plant them long ago. Joseph's gift made these two boys feel akin to the people lying under the sun-dappled green sod.

Job sat down on one of the weathered slabs to rest, and ran his fingers over the almost extinguished name and date:

1790—1851
Here lies Joshua J. Stephens
Who died of bilious fever.

The Stephens family must have died out, for they seemed to have been forgotten by all except

the twins, who visited the graves so frequently they felt intimate and on speaking terms with the dead.

"Joseph, take your foot off that baby Lilah's grave. She wouldn't like it," ordered Job.

"Baby Lilah wouldn't mind none. She'd say, 'Go right ahead, Joseph, and rest yourself,'" replied Joseph in a tone that made him always seem right with spirits and the dead.

Job felt some resentment at always having to give in, so he replied bravely, "Well, while you rest, I'm gonna collect some lizards for old Neptune's daughter, Emma Jones!"

"What you gonna do that for, Job? You know your Ma wouldn't like for you to fool with that root-workin', it's evil," said Joseph, alarmed.

"Joseph, you're just scared," jeered Job. "I don't see no harm in giving these to her. Didn't she help old Ezra out once?"

"Just the same," warned Joseph, "your Mama would sure skin your hide if she caught you dealing with old Emma Jones. Didn't we see the tree behind her house with lizard skins tacked up and drying to use in her wicked medicine? You'd better stay away and a far piece away from her root doctorin'."

All on the island had known old Emma Jones to be a root-worker for the devil. When a person wanted to do some mean and low trick to another, they would go to her with a "track" (a possession) of the person they wished her to work evil on, and she would "meager" it (cast a spell). Bessie saw her once go to a wicked person's grave and pay three brass pennies to him by burying the pennies in the back of the grave. Then she talked to the wicked spirit and told him what she wanted him to do. Emma saw Bessie watching her and swore she'd "get her even." That was long ago and Bessie, being a good common living woman and a hard worker who was royal among white and black people alike, had come to no harm. Folks claimed that Emma was so bad the boogerman was gonna catch her on top of the ground.

Despite all this and the warning from Joseph, Job went along the wall catching lizards sleeping in sun patches, until he had half dozen or more tied in his red bandanna handkerchief. He had no notion of giving them to Emma, for he too was

afraid of her conjuring, but he wanted Joseph to think him brave.

The more he collected, the more uneasy Joseph became, and he urged, "Job, Job, let's go home, let's go. You ought not be acting so biggity."

Job sat on the wall leisurely swinging his feet. Then he replied, "Just because you can see spirits and I can't, and you talk to them and I can't, ain't no sign I'm afraid of them or old Neptune's daughter neither—cause I ain't!"

"Cause you ain't what?" came a dry voice behind them. The boys froze with fright.

"You ain't afraid, are you?" The tall figure that belonged to the voice stepped over the wall. It was old Emma Jones herself! Job and Joseph had never seen her close before; her eyes were bright with evil and her lean body caved in like a grave.

"Well, what you got in your kerchief?" She reached her long skinny arm out for it, and Job was compelled to place it in her crafty fingers.

"Thank you, boys. Just what I've been looking for." With that she gave a crackling chuckle and stepped over the wall, melting again into the shadows.

After some moments they were able to speak. Joseph was furious with Job for bringing such misery upon them.

"Job, see what you've done! She is gonna conjure us, *you* especially."

"Well, said Job stubbornly, "I ain't scared, and I still don't see no harm in just givin' things away."

"Yes, but she got your track and will go to root-working on you," insisted Joseph.

They both got up on wobbly legs and took the shortcut home, going faster as they gained strength until fine sand was flying in dust clouds from their heels, and they were running full speed ahead.

The sun was low and ominous like a red ball of fire when they rounded the palmetto bank and reached their house where Bessie was sitting rocking on the porch, half asleep after her hard day's work.

"You're mighty late and you look scared," said Bessie. "What've you two been up to now?"

"Nothin', Mama, we were just running," panted Joseph.

"Well, go in and find your supper on the stove,

I'm too tired to get it for you since you're so late, then come and tell me what's been after you."

Joseph, aware that this was still a good day for spirits, said "Mama, you'd better come inside and stop nodding on the porch, some spirits are likely to be around to bother you."

"Oh, spirits! That's what's been after you! Well, go along, they won't be bothering me none this evenin'," said Bessie.

The twins had almost finished their supper when their Mother came into the house rather quickly.

"What's happened, Mama?" they asked.

"Lordy, children," answered Bessie, "While I was nodding, I heard something laugh, sorta like a hen cackling. I looked around and there was something peepin' around the corner at me, going crackle-crackle, crackle. Joseph, go out and look and see if you can see who."

Joseph went out and returned and agreed, "Yes'm, I heard them crackling and saw them peeping same as you." He was afraid old Emma had followed them home but could not be sure, and bravely added, "Guess this will teach you a lesson not to go nodding on the porch in the evening." And it did.

Work Day

Job and Joseph were awakened by Bessie counting out the clothes. "Job child," she called, where is your red bandanna?"

Job's thoughts squirmed for an excuse.

"He might've left it at the graveyard, Mama," replied Joseph coming to his rescue.

"You boys are the most no-caring children I ever saw about your clothes. Where you gonna leave them next? Graveyard! Well, I'm expecting you to find it—graveyard or no—spirits or no. It's the third one your Pa bought you from the store this month. You oughta be ashamed," scolded Bessie.

"I am," replied Job, and that he truly was. He had dreamed of lizard skins and Emma's bony hands all night and arose not feeling so well and wondering if he was being conjured. The terrible encounter with old Neptune's daughter they had experienced the day before could not be cast aside.

"You boys get out of here and help your Pa with the wood and water for my wash-in'," ordered Bessie.

The boys went out, still heavy with sleep, and the bright sunlight made their eyes blink. Big Jo was laying his ax aside a pine stump, knocking out lightwood knots, singing. He stopped and called to the boys.

"Come here, you boys, and get this "light-ard" to build your Ma's fire while I hitch up Robert and go to the field and plow. It's planting time right now. When you boys finish helping your Ma, come out and I'll show you how to plant potato slips."

Bessie called from the door, "While you twins get the pots to boiling I'll get the washing together.

Job and Joseph busied themselves collecting the chips and splitting the fat pine kindling. They started the fire under the pots and soon the water was boiling and the coals red with heat.

Joseph had observed that ever since Job got up he was cross and tired, so he asked suspiciously, "How you feeling, Little Job?"

"Oh," replied Job, "I'm feelin' tolerable."

"You mean you are feeling *bad*," insisted Joseph.

"No I ain't. I'm just feeling tolerable and nothin' more," said Job, trying to appear casual.

"You don't suppose the conjurin's started working yet, do you, little Job?" whispered Joseph.

"Hush your mouth, Joseph. Here comes Mama," said Job, irritated at Joseph suggesting something he already feared but dared not face.

They saw a huge bundle of white move along the top of the palmetto bank, then Bessie appeared around the corner carrying the clothes with ease on her head.

"Come here, you two, and help me sort out these clothes," ordered Bessie. She opened the sheets on the ground, and they put the colored clothes in one pot and the white ones in another. She stirred them with a long smooth stick, and as she stirred she hummed a song, the boys join-

ing in. Wash day at their house was a singing day,
for when Bessie worked she sang, and worked all
the better for the singing. She began with one of
their favorites while the boys accompanied her
with syncopated clapping. Before the song was
half through they broke into a lively dance around
the pots.

> *Jes from de kitchen, shoe le long,*
> *Wid a board full of biscuit, shoe le long,*
> *O Miss Mary, shoe le long,*
> *Git from de kitchen, shoe le long,*
> *Shoe le, shoe le, shoe le long!*

Soon half the wash was on the line. Bessie put their lunch with Big Joe's in a paper bag and they trotted off down the patch to the shade to eat. They came to the edge of the field and stopped to view Big Joe's and Robert's work: row after row furrowed deep in the rich black earth. The fragrance of the fresh sod reached their nostrils and they sniffed it in with spring hunger.

"Looks like Robert's on his good behavior," observed Joseph. "He always acts nice when he's plowing, but he just ain't no visiting mule."

"He sure ain't," agreed Job, "and I wish we could break him of it."

"He will one of these days," prophesied Joseph.

"Maybe," answered Job, with some doubt.

When Big Joe saw the boys, he dropped the lines and came across the field toward the children, calling, "What you boys got for my dinner?"

They sang in chorus, "Cincinnati-fried-chicken-and-hot-biscuit!"

"Um-um!" Big Joe smacked his lips and sat down beside them, mopping his forehead.

They all ate heartily; when the meal ended they had a full, comfortable feeling. Big Joe catnapped while the boys leisurely refilled their buckets with cool sulphur-smelling water from the artesian well. When they were ready to start to work, "Come here," said Big Joe, "and I'll show you how to plant taters."

Everybody knew what a growing hand Big Joe had. The boys had witnessed him plant cabbage beginning at dawn before the sun was hot, and by noon he had seven thousand, four hundred plants in the ground. As fast as Bessie could drop them for him he planted. Job and Joseph hoped to plant as well some day.

Big Joe took an apron full of slips showing the boys just how deep and how far apart to plant, dropping them on the beds about a foot apart pushing them into the earth with a notched-end stick, until they were buried two or three inches deep. After the demonstration he went back to cross-plow the corn patch and the twins began planting. Job had forgotten his ailing feeling and fear of being conjured. They experienced the same satisfaction their parents had known from years and years of labor with the soil when they

felt the warmth of the soft growing dirt enter their fingers and creep upward to store heat and strength in their bodies. They grew stronger.

After planting two long rows, they began to jump "jumping jack fashion" to stretch their cramped legs, singing:

> *Whar you goin' buzzard?*
> *Whar you goin' crow?*
> *Goin' down to de new ground*
> *To knock Jim Crow.*
> *Up to my kneecap,*
> *Down to my toe,*
> *Every time I jump up*
> *I knock Jim Crow.*

Big Joe's bass voice came to them from across the field as they clapped their hands under their knees and then touched their toes as they hopped.

They resumed their work and toiled faithfully until the ground assigned to them was new with living slices of potato they had firmly planted in the earth. Big Joe had finished plowing and joined them to help with the last row, while Robert stood blandly looking on and resting.

The shadows were slanting in the field when Bessie came out to see what they had accomplished and to tell them supper was ready.

After viewing the results, she said, "You boys sure did a fine day's work. We'll have all the vittles we can eat and some to jar up and sell besides. Praise the Lord your Pa is so strong!"

"You're strong too, Mama," admired Job.

"Yes," said Bessie, "but not half as strong as I used to be when I was a girl. I could pick cotton, great Lord! Three hundred and eighty-seven pounds was my high, and it was not hard to me with a made-up mind. I started at seven and was done at five, singing and picking with jokes and fun! When Mr. Fred needed an extra hand he'd call me. 'Bessie Boy,' he'd say, 'Lend us a hand with this bale.' Um! I was strong and I knew it and I didn't care!"

"That's right," said Big Joe, "Your Ma was a sight in the cotton field. She could out-pick any of them. Lord! How Sunny Sue hated for you to beat her picking! We would sing all day long!" Big Joe broke into the familiar cotton picking song and they all joined in while the boys danced.

Chillun, chillun
Pick a bale o' cotton
Chillun, chillun
Pick a bale o' cotton
Gwiner tote hit to de gin
Pick a bale o' cotton
Gwiner tote hit to de gin
Pick a bale o' cotton
O Lord! Pick a bale o' cotton.

"That's right," said Bessie. "Your Pa and I have spent most of our days in the field raising things for us and other folk to eat. We raised this land on our arms, and praise the Lord it's ours!" She made a gesture of lifting a heavy load Heavenward. Her arms were strong. The feeling was so deep-rooted that the little family watching were compelled to follow her movement. The four stood with raised arms looking at their field and to the Lord somewhere beyond the cypress tops.

Bessie led her singing family back into their house which stood quietly under the protecting arms of great liveoak trees and dripping moss. The roof was patched green by tiny resurrection ferns,

25

and the chimney opening safely guarded by four red clay witches balls.

Soon she had the boys fed and tucked in bed, but though Little Job was tired through and through, he lay awake watching trouble from the day before march across his mind.

Fish Day

The wind blew clear and straight from the South. Word had come from the mainland that the river was running low and great shining white-bellied shad were leaping up from the sea to spawn in the fresh black waters of the Altamaha. All of Spring surged over Big Joe as he gathered his trammel nets and prepared to head, on the morrow, for the mainland, to fish the mysterious slow-moving river, as he did each year at shad-time. He would be glad to go where spring came easy, there was none of the disquieting sweetness he felt now that had invaded the Island and taken possession of the swamp near his home.

He had promised the boys that they could go with him to set the river nets and return to a full day's fishing at sea. They planned to row to the oyster beds which lay off shore on a thin bar of sand that cut the sea-sky horizon.

Big Joe was up long before day straightening his nets and getting his fishing things together. He awakened the boys singing:

> Fishin', fishin',
> Oh, you boys goin' fishin',
> Well, den, rise,
> Rise befo' de sun
> Catches you by de toes

Big Joe yanked their toes. They tumbled out of bed and hurriedly dressed. The room danced in the firelight as did their hearts with the beginning of the longed-for day. Bessie fed them a good hot breakfast and buttoned their sweaters to their chins, for the wind before dawn was cold and high and full of salt.

The children collected their nets and baskets and bits of chicken entrails Bessie had saved for crab bait and went into the fading night where Big Joe awaited them. As they disappeared down the sand road Bessie called, "God bless you and care for you, and don't get yourself into no trouble."

The day came in from the sea now, spreading slowly from a thin line of gold, pushing darkness from every corner of the island and flooding it with light. Big Joe and the boys followed the river path to the swirling pools on the mainland where shad lay. They munched the cornpones Bessie had tucked in their pockets as they went and watched the soft willow-green blow across the water, and the feathery tops of cypress curl against the sky.

Big Joe stopped to study the deep black waters and to decide upon the best pool to set his gill net to catch shad swimming upstream. He found one to his liking and tied an end of the net to a strong bush on the bank. The other, already attached to a pole, he anchored halfway across the river, then swam back and climbed on the bank to dry in the sun. They left the net standing until night when he would return for the catch.

The day moved on and the sun became warmer —it was a day right for fishing. When they arrived where the mouth of the river emptied into the sea they found Willis, John, and Jerry already casting great spiderweb casting nets into the breakers. Big Joe rolled up his overalls and waded out near them, carrying his net over his shoulder. With one skilled swing he threw it far out, lasso-fashion, and watched it spread to form a perfect circle, then sink into the sea. Hand over hand he pulled the rope which was tied from the center of the net to his wrist, which trapped the silvery fluttering fish. With each cast the sea yielded small baitfish, shrimp, and many curious things that the boys wanted to keep, but their father forbad it claiming it was not right to take life which was not needed, and they kept only the ones they could use. The sea gave bountifully and before long they had enough.

Big Joe toted the croaker sack full of bait to their boat tied in the mouth of the river, while the boys lowered their baskets and watched the big slow-moving crabs creep into the trap after the bait. Soon they had a sack full which they tied and put into the bottom of the boat.

Finally their father made a welcome announcement, "Let's eat dinner, then head for the oyster beds and fish in the deep waters off shore." The three sprawled on the hot sand and each opened his paper bag in which Bessie had placed biscuits, side meat a'plenty, and a bitter orange. It tasted good.

Big Joe took his usual noon nap while the boys collected tiny shells on the beach and strung them on a string for Bessie. They strolled along the mud bank bordering the marsh to look for 'coon oyster. Once their father brought home a 'coon whose paw had been caught by an oyster when he had slipped down at low tide to feed upon periwinkles, fiddlers, and crabs. If Big Joe had not come along just then, the incoming tide would have drowned the little fellow, for "the oyster held him fast and wouldn't turn him loose."

After a while Big Joe called the boys to return to the boat. They climbed in the stern while their father unhitched and shoved off. He poled past the mouth of the river, laid his hands upon the oars, gathered his strength, and with one strong stroke shot the boat across the water out into the sea. The boat felt light to his touch as he dipped the oars into the foamy water. The sun was high and hot and the boys had cast aside their sweat-

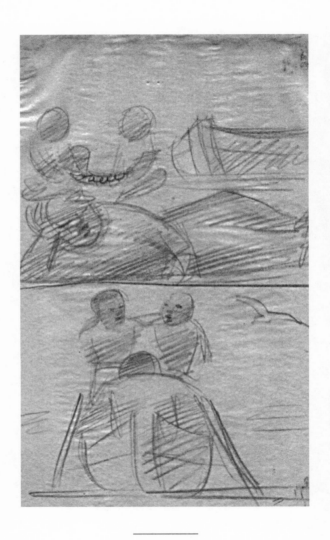

ers and sat straight-backed, barefooted, enjoying the salt spray cooling to their skins.

It would take time to reach the sandbar for it was far out in the sound, and they stopped from time to time to pull in the troll lines. The world lay cradled in a sparkling sea of blue, quiet except for the rhythmic plunge of Big Joe's oars. Stirred to this wordless music, a song began to move within him and press against his closed lips until the sound of humming was heard, then words leapt like light upon the water swelling in full sound over the sea. It made the children beat their feet upon the bottom of the boat as their father's song became part of them, the song which he had learned from his father, and he from his. It surged from within him through every rippling muscle and accelerated the beating oars like dark drums against the boat, echoing in the distance.

Suddenly as if a great bird had flown or a swift wind had blown his song away it ceased and he jerked his head upward looking full-faced into the sky. Once he had found God while singing and never let Him go. The man was glad in his heart. He recalled that plenty of things had caused him to stumble—he was a strong man with easy ways. He had been attracted to the Blue-Inn, wicked with sin-songs and dancing, but when he married Bessie she made him promise not to go there any more. He kept his word easily under her watchful eye. She had taught him to grow humble and to walk in the ways of the Lord, and to fill his lungs with song. He was proud of Bessie, tall and dark-skinned with a way of walking and a way of talking that he could not forget. Her song had caught in his throat so he married her and brought her home to the island, where soon she, too, became part of it and its folk.

Suddenly these quiet thoughts were interrupted by a scream from little Job, "Hep! Hep! Pa! Pa! Pa!"

Big Joe turned to see his son sprawled on his back, his foot in the air and a huge crab dangling from his toe. Joseph had tucked his feet under him just in time to escape the same fate. "Wait. Sit still. I'll get you loose," commanded his father. He pried the crab's claw open and dipped Little Job's toe into the stinging sea water, then he dried his tears and took off his own bandanna to wrap the toe. He ordered Job to count from fifty back to three to stop the bleeding as it instructed in the sixteenth chapter and the sixty-second verse of Ezekiel.

The bottom of the boat was now alive with crabs. Big Joe scolded as he returned them to the sack. "You boys ought to tied the knot tight. Next time I'm going to let all the crabs get you if you don't do a better job."

Their father resumed the rowing and once more the calm of the sea returned to the occupants of the boat. The white strip of sand where the oysters bedded had grown wider and longer as they reached their destination. Big Joe took the oyster rake and hauled in great hunks. The sun had already passed the mark for them to turn back, so the boys leaned over the side to help pull the heavy mat of shells into the boat. Little Job tugged once too hard and fell head downward into the sea. Before he had time to strangle, his father grabbed him by the heels and sat him upright, unharmed, but dripping wet and frightened.

"Sure as you're born, old Emma's conjuring started working," whispered Joseph in Little Job's ear.

"It ain't no such thing," objected little Job, yet he feared the worst.

"Well," insisted Joseph, "ain't the crab done bit you and nobody else? Ain't the waters done reached up and pulled you down and tried to drown you and nobody else? Its Emma Jones' root-workin' for sure! Joseph shook his head sadly over his brother's ill fate.

Little Job's heart sank, he had feared this ever since his dream. The sun had been hot and his head hurt, and now he was wet and chilled and his throat dry. He felt *bad*. Big Joe noticed the water standing in his son's eyes and asked, "Son, what's the matter, you tuckered out?"

"I sure is, Pa," he replied, holding back his tears.

"Well," comforted his father, "we'll soon be home with fish and hush-puppies for us all to eat." Their mouth watered. Bessie made hush-puppies better than anyone. They had watched her many times mix freshly ground cornmeal, bits of onion, salt and water, and drop little pones into the deep fish fat to fry. The twins liked them better than the fish itself.

Soon Big Joe had as many oysters as the boat could carry. He announced it was time to start in. On the way the "putt-putt" engines of the little shrimp fleet passing, straining under their heavy load, was cheery and businesslike—the sound of a satisfactory day at sea. Job and Joseph watched the sea gulls follow the boats and dart down to steal bits of shrimp and fish entrails while the men in the stern cleaned their catch on the way in to the fish market.

When they reached the pier, Big Joe unloaded the boat and carried the fish up to the market. Soon he returned smiling at the boys, "You sure brought me luck this day! The most I've made in five catches! You two are as good help as one man right now and someday, before too long, will own your own boat." This bit of praise from their father pleased the twins, for Big Joe was sparing with his words.

The boys' legs wobbled as they neared home. They were weary with the man-sized day. When they came in sight of the house, they saw Bessie rush out waving something in her hand. When she neared them they saw it was a red bandanna. She was excited and gathered Little Job in her arms crying, "Thank the Lord my baby is safe!"

"Course he's safe," said Big Joe, "Why'd you take on so for?" Bessie ignored him and asked Little Job, "Are you all right, baby? Are you? Tell your Ma!"

"What's the matter with you, Bessie?" demanded Big Joe, realizing something terrible must be wrong.

"Well," began Bessie, "I was passing Black Bank Creek at the upper end near old Emma Jones' house. She saw me and come out waving Little Job's bandanna at me. She said, 'Bessie Proctor, here's your boy's bandanna.' I said, 'where'd you get it, Emma Jones?' She said, 'He done give it to me.' I said, 'He wouldn't do no such thing; he don't make truck with your kind.' And she said, 'He *did*. And he ain't biggity like his Ma neither, but I don't like none of you Proctors, so you better watch out!' Then she flip Job's bandanna in my face and spit on the ground and make a mark. I snatched it from her and flipped it back at her and said, 'You'd better not start none of your dirty root-

working on my baby. Before God, I mean it, too!"
Bessie had related the incident without stopping
to catch her breath. Then she continued.

"She don't like my chance in life. She wants to
fix my baby cripple and take all we have and more
too for doctors. Then we would be down under
the feet of people with nothin'! She walks foot-
and-foot with the devil. She's the devil workin' on
land!"

Little Job clung to his Mama and sobbed, com-
pletely exhausted and frightened. Now he knew
that he was in for a big dose of conjuring.

Big Joe set the fish down and picked the little
boy up in his arms, carried him into the house and
laid him trembling on the bed for Bessie to un-
dress.

Joseph followed wailing in a high screech voice,
"Trouble, trouble, trouble done come to our house!

The Conjurer's Spell

All night Bessie prayed and tended Little Job. She put cold cloths on his head and bricks soaked in hot vinegar at his feet. Little Job tossed and rolled his eyes back in his head and didn't say "nothin'."

"Oh Lord!" prayed Bessie, "Save my baby from Emma Jones' root-workin'. I know you is stronger than the devil she works for, and I'm your servant. Do something for our baby, Jesus! Yes, Lord, do something. You been my family doctor and kept your strong arm around me all these days, deliver us from the hands of our enemy. I mean! Bless my family as you did Noah's, take us into your Ark. I know you can save him—you've healed the blind, raised up the dead, busted tombstones—so save my baby. Great Lord! If anything does happen to my baby I sure am gonna put a stop to Emma Jones. She's just too far wrong, that's all. So keep my hands from wrong and save this house from shame. Show me how to cure my baby, Oh, Lord! My Jesus! Amen."

Big Joe was as worried as Bessie, but he sat silent by the fire all night to keep it going and the water hot. Neither slept.

The night was long and Little Job's sleep disturbed. He would cry out, "Lizards' skins, Mama! Lizards after me!"

Bessie would comfort him and say, "Now, baby, here's your Ma, don't fret, there ain't no lizards, your Pa done killed them all."

Finally Little Job sank into a deep sleep. So deep Bessie kept leaning over him to see if he was still breathing. She couldn't help thinking what a pretty angel Baby Job would make lying there in his little white gown looking so innocent. "Sure with white wings and a gold harp he'd be a sight for Jesus!" She could see Jesus lowering his chariot by his bed to give Little Job a ride. She controlled her thoughts with effort and said aloud, "He got to live, Lord, my baby is too little

to die. He'd make a no-count angel, anyhow Lord."

The night was long and day crept slowly through the cracks. Big Joe went out for more wood and Bessie made coffee. The days slipped by unheeded by Little Job, who lay staring at the ceiling, not eating, and sleeping only fitfully. He complained to his Mama that "little old men come in and bother me," so much so that they rooted him out of his bed one night and Bessie had to make a pallet on the floor. She feared the cotton mattress was not good for his fever.

Neighbors sent food and kept their table well supplied. Some sent bits of string and horsehair, some blue ground glass with flakes of dried skin, one a rabbit's hind foot, all hoping one would break the conjurer's spell. A few like Aunt Pearl and Julie came and helped Bessie tend Little Job, but the rest stayed away for fear of entering a house with the hex on it. Aunt Julie, seeing Bessie's suffering, said "The price of Death ain't what you're expectin' it to be."

Joseph visited around the neighborhood and acted out their encounter with old Emma Jones, scattering the big-eyed children, making them run to hide behind their mama's skirts, only to be tempted and to return the next day to be frightened again, as Joseph made his tale increasingly vivid and gruesome.

Big Joe's heart was heavy, he was silent and his work went undone. Robert stood idle and sullen in his stall. Baby Job seemed to be wasting away in front of their eyes in spite of all they could do.

Big Joe remarked to Bessie, "Look like he can't walk, he can't talk, he can't sit up, he can't stand. Seem to me he getting ready to go off on the train."

Bessie did not give up, and on the seventh day of his illness she prayed all night. With the dawn, came a knock at the door. Big Joe opened it. A stranger standing there said, "A boy named Job live in this house."

"Yes, that's right," confirmed Big Joe.

Bessie came forward and said, "Come in stranger. You're come from the Lord to save our baby!"

"I am," said the man. He walked over and stood for a moment looking down at Little Job. Then he put his finger between his eyebrows and commanded, "Boy, sit up."

For a moment Job did not move, then he slowly sat erect.

"Now, boy, stand!" commanded the stranger.

Job stood.

"Good," said the stranger, "The Lord is workin' His mighty hand." He laid little Job down and covered him up and turned to Bessie. "Have the boy ready when I come to get him this night at twelve, the moon will be right."

With that he went outside and walked around the house three times. When he left, a peace, which had not been there for a long time, stayed behind and Bessie knew that Little Job would get well.

The rest of the afternoon Bessie saw signs of her boy's improvement. He drank a little pot-liquor. Joseph came in, mightily relieved to see his brother better. Besides, he was tried of his own stories and of frightening the neighborhood children, and wanted Little Job up and well again to play with him.

Joseph leaned over the bed and said "You better get well Little Job, there's a carnival comin' to town. Please get well before Saturday and then Pa will take us and we can ride on the Merry-go-round and eat cotton candy. Get well," he urged, "cause I wants us to go."

Little Job looked at him and smiled for the first time since he had been stricken, but he said nothing.

"What's that you promising Baby Job?" inquired Big Joe.

"Nothing, Pa, except you most likely to take us to the carnival if he gets well before Saturday," explained Joseph.

"I will for sure, and be rejoicing to do so," promised Big Joe.

A little before the stranger was to return at midnight, Bessie dressed Little Job warmly and wrapped him in a blanket and set him by the fire. They all waited.

Finally buggy wheels were heard outside. The stranger appeared at the door dressed in a black suit with tails and a tall silk hat. He picked the child up in his arms and carried him out into the night without speaking. He gave a shrill whistle and off they rode into the darkness.

The Cure

Little Job watched the horse head straight for the mainland, the marshes flying by blurred in the night. It seemed to him an endless time before his companion announced, "Job, we is here." He turned the horse's head down a faint path through a field to the foot of a small hill. He drove the buggy around the mound three times, stopped, then seven more, stopped. He got out and carried Little Job up the path. When they reached the top, Job saw it was a graveyard with many curious things on each grave, bits of glistening glass, unusual bottles set in rows, and many household belongings, including a porcelain chamber pot. The stranger set Little Job on a slab with a

pair of great ram horns at the head. It was an old doctor's grave—a good man like the stranger.

He commanded Little Job to sit straight and look ahead and to never look back. Job stared straight ahead fearing if he looked back he would turn into a pillar of salt like someone in the Bible. He watched the tops of the tall cedar trees pierce the sky like great black witches' hats. But he did not move.

The stranger walked the graves and stopped at the head of the one where Little Job sat. A slip of moon was rising over the edge of the world and the silence was heavy. Wind blew across the marshes, through the field, and danced up the hill. The silence was suddenly shattered as the stranger spoke, words poured from his lips in an unknown tongue, mutterings and mighty rumblings accompanied the words Little Job could not understand. Then the stranger called the dead and said, "I have a boy here who is fixed with an evil spirit. I ask you, in Jesus' name, can and will you cure him? If so, give me a sign."

A queer noise like the deep groan of a man awakening came from the depths of the grave.

The stranger said, "I will pay you the sum of ten percent in silver to cure him, and promise me."

The same noise was heard again. Then the stranger stooped down and dug into the head of the grave up to his elbow and put ten pieces of old silver in the hole. Then he took some clay from the bottom of the hole and stood over Job's head.

He began to talk rapidly and soon was accompanied by a wild beating on something that sounded like a hollow wooden drum. Little Job felt the sound surround him, consume him; it came from no one place but from everywhere. The sick heaviness left him and he felt light as if suspended in midair, and wondered if he were dead or dreaming or yet alive. He was tempted to look down to see if he still had a body but he was afraid to lower his eyes, so he sat stone-still staring straight ahead as he had been bidden and floated in a world of sound. His leg turned cold, cold, cold.

As suddenly as the noise began, it stopped. The night was thick with silence. There was a long wait. The black figure of the stranger appeared before him silhouetted against the sky. He made a low bow and said, "Thank you Cura Masheen," as if to say "Well done."

Then he stretched his long arm toward Little Job and beckoned with a crooked finger, saying, "Come Job, stand."

Little Job slowly stood. His feet felt like no feet at all. "Take a step," commanded the stranger, his eyes burning through the darkness. Little Job stepped.

"Step again," he repeated. As the child stepped forward, the stranger stepped back still beckoning. Little Job felt his body return, his feet became feet again and sure on the ground, until he was running toward the stranger who caught and lifted him high into the buoyant air and twirled him around. Then he sat Little Job down, holding him by the hand, and together they walked down the hill to the buggy.

The ride back was without words as was the ride to the graveyard, but for a different reason. Little Job felt strong, strong as his Mama when she was a girl. Strong enough to kill himself a spirit if he'd known which one had done the trick to him. He knew that he was well and no amount of conjurin' could ever make him ill again. He wondered if the Holy Ghost had entered his body. His leg was well but it felt different, as it was to feel different for the rest of his natural life. He wished he could sit in Jesus' lap and tell Him all about it and thank him for all He had done to help him.

Bessie, Big Joe, and Joseph heard the buggy wheels turn down their road and went out on the porch to greet them. The stranger stopped long enough for Little Job to jump down and run to his Mama's outstretched arms. Then he cracked his whip and disappeared into the flaming dawn.

Saturday

Saturday they arose with much rejoicing. The sun was high, for those inside the blue-shuttered house with red clay witches' balls on the chimney corners had slept long and well. Breakfast was a feast Bessie had prepared for the occasion, before awakening the household. It consisted of fresh eggs, grits, a piece of side-meat, hot biscuits, and bitter-orange marmalade which she had made from the wild oranges on the island. Little Job ate almost as much as his father, which made Big Joe laugh and say, "If you eat like that, you gonna have to get a job at the builders with me to help pay for your vittles."

Big Joe worked three days a week and half day on Saturday. Everyone knew him to be the finest carpenter and pipe layer in the crew, and besides, he was the best hand to drive a truck. Mr. Ivy wanted Big Joe to work every day but he refused because he liked to tend his farm and to catch fish, so Mr. Ivy arranged the work to suit Big Joe.

As soon as breakfast was over he left for work saying, "Boys, when I get back, be ready with your Ma and we'll sure go to town this Saturday evening."

This pleased the twins for they had been working on the idea for some time. They ran around the house cutting capers and Bessie declared, "Springs in them heels again boys!" and was glad to see it there.

After she had done the breakfast dishes she sat the boys down in front of her for a lecture.

"I have an errand to do before we go anywhere. I want you two young ones to sit still and listen." They sat on the bench with their feet and hands together as they always did when Bessie stood before them with such a determined look, her hands on her hips. She continued, "You two have a mighty close call with the devil, he well-nigh rooted Baby Job out from the bed and snatched him off. Joseph, you quit grinning because you were in close danger too. I'm ashamed for both of you not having any better sense than to play with old Emma Jones and her wickedness. I want you to quit acting so biggity and so mannish. Do you understand?"

The twins nodded, still not knowing what to expect. She went on, "I've been studying all morning and part of the night what to do with you. Now I know, and I am the gladdest woman in the world!"

This puzzled the boys still more, Bessie was in too good a humor for whipping, yet they knew their sins would not go unpunished.

"I've decided," she continued, "to go right down and have a talk with Reverend Cigar King and see if he will baptize you with his crowd this very Sunday. I want him to wash away your sins if I takes two duckings and you come out a double Baptist! I want him to consecrate you to the Lord before the devil gets you for keeps. I want it done now, let no time slip, cause you two are bound to get yourselves in more trouble. Then if Death lays his icy hands on you, you'll be a good Baptist gone and I won't be wondering if you are down sizzling somewhere in the bad place, heaping coal upon coal, fire upon fire, through eternity." She noticed the gloomy look on their faces and asked, "What's the matter with you two, don't you want to be saved?"

"Yes'm," said Joseph, "but Alice she got saved and now she don't have any fun. She just sets on the porch and reads the Bible all day to her grandma."

"I'd be ashamed," said Bessie. "Besides, Alice is Alice, and you are you, and I don't intend for you to grow up into one of them door-to-door comparers, either."

"Mama, I'm afraid," said Little Job, a new idea popping into his head.

"No you ain't, now get!" ordered Bessie, putting a stop to their alibis.

Outside the yard was filled with the laughter of children who had come to see Little Job up and well, and as usual on Saturday mornings to crowd Bessie's yard. Bessie laid a restraining hand on her sons and gave them the last warning to mind their manners and to keep peace while she was on an important visiting errand to Reverend King's. They promised to behave as they wiggled loose and leapt from the porch in the midst of the fun.

The yard was in motion, a crazy-quilt motion, the pattin' and the stampin' and the shakin' began. "Come sweet child," Sue called, "and scratch your chigger, chigger bug gonna get bigger and bigger." Ben sang out in a singsong way:

Possum, possum, don't you play with me,
pretendin' to sleep in that hollow tree,
better wake up for its too late,
Mr. Polecat's walkin' in an easy gait.
Oh, Mr. Turkey, you better run,
Preacher's a'comin' and your day is done.
Ham-bone, Ham-bone and Gravy too,
chased Jane around the house
and she fairly flew.
Come on buzzard, come on crow,
hoppin' around and going just so.
Now step, oh step, oh step it down,
turn your partners, swing them around.
Rap-down boys on Saturday night,
Rap-down boys on Saturday night,
your dress is red, your shoes is white,

gotta get to town this Saturday night
Now Emma called a game to play,
String them beans lady, string them fast . . .
you gonna be my wife at last.

When Bud went down he went down hard, so did every child in the yard, they crawled around like Mr. Snake then rose on their tails eating wedding cake. Ned called out "God the buzzard in my feet, hopped around the old dead cow picking his bones and showing 'em how." Big Boy picked up and beat the tin pan, rattled them bones and the fun began. Jepp spread down his red bandanna, folded the corners, threw it on his love, she did the same, a high steppin' game. "Emma's bawlin' the Jack till her Honey comes back. Rip's got the jitters and the jerks, let's clap for him boys till he falls in the dirt. Booger, booger, booger, you stealing in the yard, no fair cheatin' Jos makin' hit hard. No fun hidin' behind the hen house do'. Now count ten—let's go!" All of them stopped playing to watch Josephine shout, "Shout Josephine, shout, shout, now rock the baby, sweet sweet sweet, Oh Johnny Hoe-Cake eat, eat."

When Bessie returned she sang a jump-up song

and the children jumped and jumped high and long. When they were all out of breath and quiet she said, "Now get! So many children under foot I can't laugh, I can't sing, I can't pray. Clear out, children, 'cause I've got work to do!" The children knew she meant it and scattered like wild geese leaving Job and Joseph to face their determined-looking Mother.

Bessie took the twins inside to hear the result of her special mission. "Well," she began, "I walked up to Reverend King's house and he's sitting on the porch in a white palm beach suit. He said, 'Holy greetings in Jesus' name, Sister Bessie. What can I do for you?' I said, 'Reverend, I've come to get you to save my boys. I want you to baptize them right off. Little Job has a close call with the Devil. He wrestled with him for a week—but the Lord won out.' 'Amen,' said the Reverend. Then he said, 'Be patient with children, Bessie, 'cause they're coming and you're going and what you say is coming up in them. If you lie or if you say what's good it sticks with them when they grow up. It's inside them. Bring your boys down, Bessie, in the morning, where the big River empties into the sea. I've a crowd of sinners to baptize and we start at dawn. I'll sure be happy to save them, Sister Bessie.' Then I said, 'Thank you, Reverend this day, I will have them there and a full-grown chicken, too, for your Sunday dinner.'"

"Now, Mama, can we get ready to go with Pa to town?" they asked, having heard their fate settled.

"Sure," answered Bessie, "but first you come here and let me wash you good. Lord, but you're dirty and you grow like weeds!" She shook her head wisely over the mighty workings of the Lord and gave the boys a good scrubbing. She scrubbed so hard they thought their skins had come off so they ran to the mirror only to see their skins still on and nice and clean and shiny.

Bessie dressed them in crisp suits and polished shoes that pinched, new straw hats, and was more than proud of their appearance when she looked them over.

"If your Pa can see you while you are clean he'll see how pretty them hats fit your face. So sit still while I get dressed," she ordered.

Soon Big Joe arrived and changed his clothes

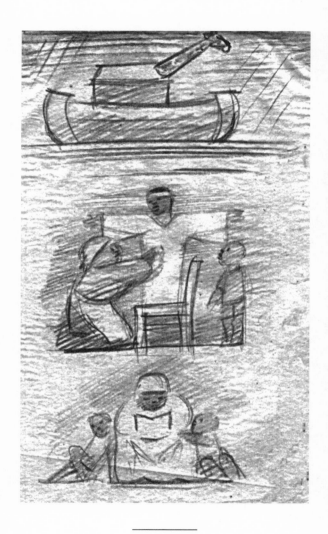

for a pink-striped shirt—stiff with starch—Bessie had laid out for him. When they were all ready to set forth to town, Big Joe looked at his neat little family and was satisfied.

On the edge of town they saw wagons standing, mules unhitched and tied. "Lots of folk come," observed Bessie. "Sure," said Big Joe, "been coming since morning. Look at them chairs in the wagons, must've brought all their family and neighbors, too."

They turned down the main street and saw a huge crowd around the carnival that consisted of a Merry-go-round, a tent that concealed wild animals, and a few stands where vendors sold goobers, popcorn, and cotton candy. The boys looked like jumping jacks as they bobbed up and down with excitement, saying, "Look, Mama! Look, Papa! Look!"

Bessie and Big Joe knew everyone. He claimed "friends would meet where dollars wouldn't." Their progress to the tent was slow because they stopped at each group to shake hands. Finally they arrived at the cotton candy machine. Big Joe bought the biggest cones the man offered for the boys and they enjoyed the way it melted like sweetspun air as their lips touched it. They smacked their lips and let each bite be a special and complete delight in itself.

Big Joe bought tickets to the Merry-go-round. Joseph mounted a fiery steed with a red tongue and red saddle. Job picked a white stallion with mane and tail like sea foam and a saddle of blue and gold, while Bessie and Big Joe sat in the golden chariot. Bessie wondered if it was like the heavenly chariot in the Bible. The horses bobbed up and down to the calliope music, and the twins galloped off into a bright and shiny world they had not known before. When the music and the Merry-go-round stopped, the twins clung to their steeds and refused to dismount. Bessie and Big Joe had to grab one apiece and pull them off bodily. "What're you acting up so for, Job?" Bessie scolded. "We want to ride again." they begged. "What you think your Pa's pockets is lined with, gold? Well, they ain't!" If you wanta see the wild animals you'd better behave right now," she warned.

The Barker was in the midst of a marvelous tale

about man-eating tiger and the cobra inside the tent. " See all for fifteen cents!" His descriptions made the boys shudder with fear and delight at the same time. Big Joe bought each a ticket and they went inside where the first thing they saw were the tall, pink glasses of lemonade and they started in chorus begging for some.

"Hush your mouth," ordered Bessie. "Ain't I told you your Pa wasn't made of money, you two acting like he could spit gold!"

Big Joe finally gave in, saying, "Well, I brought you in here to see the animals God made, but it looks like fifteen cent ticket gonna let you see nothing except pink lemonade, if I don't satisfy your thirst first." He bought each a tall glass of the sweet pink liquid and they gulped it down greedily. Then they turned their attention to the animals.

They were awestruck and a bit frightened and clung tightly to their parents' hands. Bessie and Joe were as curious as the boys.

"What's that, Mama?" they cried at each cage.

Bessie had taught herself to read and could read

all the familiar books of the Bible as well as Reverend King himself. Most of these names she had read in the story of Noah. "Gee-raff," she answered, "Praise the Lord! I've always wanted to see this booger!"

"Why his neck so long, Mama?" asked Job.

"I don't know except the Lord made him that way. Ain't that reason enough? When he got in the Ark Noah had to hoist the window and let him stick his neck out, because the roof was too low." She recalled the picture she had once seen of Noah's Ark with the animals all looking out the windows.

The second time around the cages the boys had gained enough courage to feed the baby monkey peanuts through the bars. Joseph stood so near the cage the mama monkey reached out and grabbed his new straw hat and tried it on. Everyone laughed, except Joseph. The monkey danced around and around until Joseph was on the verge of tears and begged "Mama, make her give it back, she gonna ruin it."

But all the persuading and coaxing was to no

avail and she plainly showed that she had no intention of giving up her new prize hat. The keeper of the animals finally came over to help.

"Come now, Floss, be a good girl, give the boy his hat." But Floss was not interested until he held up a ripe banana. Her mood changed and she rushed excitedly to the bars and held out her hands jabbering as fast as she could. "No," said the keeper, "First give me the hat." He pointed to Joseph's hat on her head and the bartering began. Finally she gave in and exchanged the hat for the banana, to Joseph's relief and the crowd's amusement.

"That's the difference between monkeys and women," the keeper philosophized, "Women will do without food to buy a hat and the monkey will give up her new hat for food . . . a funny world."

It was growing dark, the lights of the carnival were gay and the boys hated to leave when Bessie announced it was time to go home. She insisted, for she had to cut up sheets and make their baptismal robes for the Holy Event on the morrow.

When they were home, she undressed the tired little boys and gave them supper, then read a chapter in the Bible and put them to bed. They soon fell asleep with the carnival lights still dancing before their eyes and wondering what the cold, icy water in the early morning would do to their sins.

Bessie sat up late making the two little white robes and headbands for them to wear the next day.

The Baptizing

Bessie arose before the sun was up and lit the oil lamps. Her preparation for Sunday always began early and since this was a very special Sunday, she got up an hour sooner than usual.

When the preliminaries were over and breakfast was ready, she awakened the boys with, "Get up, get up angel children! It's time to eat your breakfast and get yourselves prepared to be baptized! This is your day, children, so rise and shine!"

After they had dressed in their very best clothes and eaten their "Holy Breakfast" of milk and wild honey, Bessie read to them the forty-seventh Psalm. The two little stiff, starched, white robes rattled like palmetto leaves in the wind as she slipped them over their heads and pinned the white crowns around their foreheads. Big Joe came in from hitching Robert to the wagon and said, "Ain't them boys a pretty and a Holy sight, Um-um!"

"They sure are," said Bessie, "I know this day the Lord is willing and anxious for you two to be saved and your sins washed away."

"Mama, I'm afraid," insisted Little Job.

"I told you, you ain't no such thing," retorted Bessie.

"I ain't, Mama," said Joseph, "I want to rise up out of the water shouting and hollering like I saw them do last summer at the Big Creek baptizin'."

"Mama," Job persisted, "I'm afraid the preacher will drown us."

"No such thing, you oughta be ashamed," scolded Bessie. "The Lord gave Reverent Cigar King a strong arm and power just to do this emerging. You two are to be baptized together because you were born together. Now you gotta get *re*-born together."

"How can he do that, Mama?" asked Joseph.

"He'll lay you both back across his arm and duck you at the same time. Be sure to hold your breath so you young ones don't strangle. When you come up you'll have a wondrous feeling and you'll feel the Holy Ghost enter your body and you are changed, understand, you are *changed*. Then when you come out purified, climb out on the bank to your Ma and Pa and we'll help you get into dry clothes. Now do you see?"

"Yes'm," answered Joseph.

"You, Job?" questioned Bessie.

"Yes'm, that is, I sorta do," replied Job.

"What you mean 'sorta do'? Job, don't tell me the Devil is still working on you after all you been through. You sure are a mystery, a mystery to yourself too, I do believe. The Stranger won't come again to help you, now do you understand?" demanded Bessie. "Yes'm," Little Job finally gave in.

It was time to go. Big Joe had driven Robert around to the front and was waiting for them in the wagon. He had placed two straight chairs in the back for the boys.

As they started, Bessie observed, "Um. Robert's acting mighty wise today, he must be thinking up some meanness."

"No, he just acting like a Sunday mule with religion," said Big Joe.

"That mule ain't got no religion—he spoiled rotten," said Bessie with disgust. "And if I know mules, right now he's got a notion in his mind— I don't like none of them four-legged mules."

"You acting like you ain't been raised amongst mules all you life," declared Big Joe. "Besides, Robert might've changed his ways, people do."

The boys climbed in the wagon and sat straight on their chairs.

Bessie put in the basket of food for the church dinner-on-the-ground which was to take place after the baptizing, and a fat hen for the preacher. Then she climbed in front beside Big Joe. Big Joe clucked to Robert and they started for the end of the island where the big river emptied into the sea and where the baptizing was to take place.

They were not the first to arrive, for the crowd had been gathering since before day, but they were in time, for the sun had just begun breaking in a Holy yellow light across the water.

Little Job and Joseph took their places at the head of the long line of winter converts, standing in their white robes waiting to have their sins washed away. Bessie kissed them and left them in the hands of the Lord and the Preacher, then joined Big Joe on the sandbank where they could get a good view of the mighty spectacle.

Before long, the Preacher and two deacons dressed in long black robes entered the water. The Reverend lifted his hand and silence fell upon those standing at the edge of the water and upon the waiting congregation. He led the procession slowly out until they were standing waist-deep in the river. As they walked, a beautiful song rose from their throats and "the Glory of the Lord shone round about them."

> *Lead me to de healin' water,*
> *Water, water,*
> *Lead me to de healin' water,*
> *Be baptized.*
> *Touchin' de healin' water,*
> *Water, water,*
> *Touchin' de healin' water*
> *Healed my blinded eyes.*

Down in de healin' water,
Water, water,
Down in de healin' water
Felt my spirit rise.

Mergin from de healin' waters,
Waters, waters,
Mergin from de healin' waters
De dove of peace arise.

Lifted from de healin' water,
Water, water,
Lifted from de healin' water,
By Christ my Saviour's side.

Lead me to de healin' water,
Water, water,
Lead me to de healin' water
Be baptized.

The song continued, but softly, as the Preacher lowered the converts into the water. Little Job and Joseph were first. The Reverend raised his hand and said, "I now baptize thee, my beloved twins Job and Joseph Proctor, in the name of the Father,

in the name of the Son, and in the name of the Holy Ghost." With the last words he ducked the twins before they could resist his firm grasp.

Bessie, seeing her boys disappear under the water, threw her hands up and cried, "Praise the Lord! Praise the Son! Praise the Holy Ghost!"

"Ah-men," was heard throughout the gathering.

Joseph came up shouting with his eyes rolled back, "Hallelujah! Hallelujah! I've been baptized!"

His father and mother were mighty proud of the way he took on. Bessie said "He is sure doing magnificent!" Then they looked for Little Job and to their horror he was pretending to swim out hand over hand.

"Wait till I settle with that young one!" exclaimed Bessie, as she rushed to the edge of the water and snatched him out. Removing Little Job from earshot of the congregation, she popped him on his flanks saying, "Why you act up so, disgracing your Pa and me?"

"Mama, I was just seeing if the Lord taught me to swim," yelped Job.

"You can't expect Him to do everything at one time, son. He just finished saving you and that ought to be enough to satisfy you this time," said Big Joe.

After the parents had rubbed them down with a big towel and stuffed them into dry clothes, they went back to see the rest of the baptizing.

"Look, Mama," said Little Job, "It don't look like Mr. John wants to be baptized. He keeps moving to the end of the line away from the Preacher."

"Hush, baby, he's makin' up his mind," said Big Joe.

"Well," declared Bessie, "He ought to made it up before now—but still it ain't too late, though it's late."

The Preacher baptized them one by one, and one by one they rose from the water filled with the Holy Ghost, shouting. It was a glorious sight. Sister Carrie, the worst sinner of them all who had cut her husband something terrible and banged Jessie Miller's head open for looking at him, was the most consumed. She flung her arms Heavenward and fell back stiff as a board in the Preacher's arms, rolled her eyes back until only the whites showed, and proceeded to develop the Holy jerks. The two assisting deacons carried her ashore to her brother's and sister's arms.

"She sure is cleansed now," said Bessie, "And Praise the Lord for so doing."

Finally all were baptized except Big John Pryor still standing as far as he could from the Preacher, hesitating. "Can't see what's the matter with him, he don't dance, he don't drink, he don't smoke, but it just looks like he's going to Hell on general principles," observed Bessie.

The congregation was tense, not a sound was heard. All were waiting to see which road he would take. Then Reverend King took command, "Don't jail your thoughts, Brother. Come, Sin No More!"

Suddenly there was a clean break with his conscious, no time now to spend and no need, Big John threw his sins away, strength surged through him; with his head back he walked unafraid toward the Preacher churning up the waters as he marched forward crying, "Thank you, Jesus! Thank you, Jesus!" The Preacher and the two deacons received him gladly and laid him out flat under the water. No one spoke.

The waters parted for Big John, who rose, glistening black, shining, powerful. The Preacher and the deacons moved back in wonder, a trembling fell upon those who witnessed, some knees gave way and they knelt moaning, some bowed their heads crying, then a mighty silence fell upon them all as Big John spread his hands over their heads and blessed them as he walked among the sheep. Old Mary Crow discarded her crutches and hobbled, then ran with gladness; Brazier's boy who had not spoken since he nearly drowned in the Yellow Creek talked "A witness! To the Lord!" he cried. "Ah-men" "Jesus-Jesus!" resounded through the bent-head figures.

Big John spoke, "Words from the Lord are moving in my mind. They say 'Go ye John straight to Shanty Town, smash the Willow Inn and there set up an Altar unto me and preach!" He took no time to change his clothes but walked straight ahead, his garments flying behind. All who saw him knew him to be a man chosen by God to do His bidding, and stepped aside to let him pass, except Jepp Morris, who was called to accompany him to the end. Later Jepp told how Big John, fired with God, smashed the Willow door, tore down curtains, gamblers leapt from

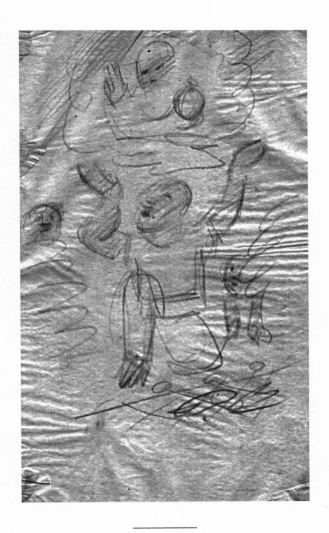

windows, women fell on their faces. He broke bottles, threw out dice, commanded gamblers to return and to build an altar to the Lord; they did his bidding. The might of his words worked wonders, and so did his strong arm, and five and ten cent pieces were dropped in his hands as he led the sinners to repent. After that the Willow Inn was a Hall of the Lord and people crowded in to hear Big John the Magnificent, preach.

The congregation, torn by such a miracle, was dazed. Gradually they were released from Big John's presence and the women turned their attention to the children and gathered the baskets of food stored in the wagons. It was late in the morning and all had eaten breakfast early and were hungry. The ladies began to unwrap the dinner and to lay it on long strips of newspaper they had placed on the ground. The table was piled high with sweet potatoes, sweet-potato pie, chickens fried, chickens stewed, and chickens baked, cold greens, collards and fine cornbread and biscuits, cakes and pies and jams and jellies—all the bounties the Good Lord could provide.

Little Job and Joseph could hardly wait until the

Preacher's long blessing was over. The parents kept their eyes on the greedy children and hands upon their collars to make sure manners came before appetites. After the food had been well blessed all who gathered sat down on each side of the table and began to eat. There was plenty for everyone, the old ones said they had never seen such a feast. When all had eaten to their fullest capacity, Reverend King rose and spoke a few words of welcome to the new members.

"Welcome unto the folds of this Church, Brothers and Sisters, welcome! This day you have witnessed a miracle of the Lord and had your sins washed away. Now you shall rise in that getting-up morning and go with us to our Heavenly Home. We know Death to be. We know Death comes to take us all. 'Be ready,' says Jesus. 'Be ready to take a ride on the train.' Those who has been baptized and ready have bought your ticket and are waitin' for the train. You gonna ride, Brother, you gonna ride, Sister, and no conductor can keep you off."

"Yes, Lord," "You said it, Jesus," responded through the congregation. The Preacher continued, "When God calls you, you will ride but don't forget Jesus' promise. He promised you gonna rise again." "Yes, yes, Lord," responded the members. "Come Sister Bessie, lead us in a rising song."

Bessie stood up and began her song. She clapped her hands and beat her foot in an alternating rhythm and the members based her:

> *Tombstone bustin'*
> *In dat gettin'-up mornin',*
> *Gettin'-up mornin',*
> *Gettin'-up mornin',*
> *Tombstone bustin'*
> *In dat gettin'-up mornin'*
> *Way over in de graveyard.*
>
> *Gonner rise shoutin' Holy*
> *In dat gettin'-up mornin',*
> *Gettin'-up mornin',*
> *Gettin'-up mornin',*
> *Gonner rise shoutin' Holy*
> *In dat gettin'-up mornin'*
> *Way over in de graveyard.*
>
> *Gonner meet King Jesus*
> *In dat gettin'-up mornin'*

Gettin'-up mornin'
Gettin'-up mornin'
Gonner meet King Jesus
In dat gettin'-up mornin'
Way over in de graveyard.

All trouble will be over
In dat gettin'-up mornin'
Gettin'-up mornin'
Gettin'-up mornin'
All trouble will be over
In dat gettin'-up mornin'
Way over in de graveyard.

Tombstone bustin'
In dat gettin'-up mornin'
Gettin'-up mornin'
Gettin'-up mornin'
Tombstone bustin'
In dat gettin'-up mornin'
Way over in de graveyard.

The singing and the clapping and the beat of feet upon the sod accelerated, a mighty joy had come to them all.

When the song was over, the congregation was

formally dismissed by a prayer from Deacon Gamble. Big Joe then went to hitch Robert to the wagon as Bessie was anxious to take the boys home and to put them to bed early while they were freshly baptized.

Bessie and the boys sat for a long time waiting for Big Joe.

"Wonder what's happened to Pa?" asked Little Job.

"Guess he's talking," answered Joseph.

"Well, if he is, he's talking to himself," said Bessie, "cause us the last ones here. Little Job, run see what's the matter."

Job soon came back calling "He ain't there, Robert gone, Pa gone, but the wagon there."

"Gone!" exclaimed Bessie. "I knew that Robert was up to something. Looks like he could pick a different day for his meanness!"

They waited and before very long they saw Big Joe coming leading Robert, who looked as innocent as the day he was born.

"Where'd you find him?" called Bessie.

"In Jail, the mule jail. Tilly. Life done locked him up and wanted ten dollars bail."

"How come? What'd Robert do?" asked Bessie, alarmed over the price.

"He damaged his cornpatch, moved in and helped himself, evidence, evidence everywhere!"

"Where'd you get ten dollar?" asked Bessie. "Borrowed on my next week's pay from Mr. Ivy," answered Big Joe. "What a shame, shame, shame," said Bessie, "but I guess we can make out—we have to as long as you insist on keeping that rotten mule!"

Big Joe hitched Robert to the wagon and they climbed in. The ride home was uneventful and the boys amused themselves by counting the egrets nesting in the big trees along the edge of the marsh. It had been a big day and all were tired. Little Job and Joseph had been good and the day was filled with excitement. When they finally turned down the road toward their house, Job remarked to his brother,

"We sure got plenty religion this day."

"We sure have," replied Joseph, "but I got mine first."

"No such thing!" argued Job, punching his brother's ribs.

"I did, too!" Joseph hit his brother back.

Blows now were being exchanged faster and harder, and before Bessie could reach back to sever the two, the chairs upset and the boys spilled upside down still pounding each other and the air between.

Big Joe pulled Robert to a halt and separated the boys, saying, "Looks like neither of you got religion this day. I've a good mind to get Reverend King to baptize you all over next Sunday."

"No, Pa, we're just playing—honest, Pa," they pleaded, fearing utter disgrace. "All right, then, but you behave like Christians, leastwise till I gets you home and out of sight of the neighbors," agreed their father.

He clucked to Robert to resume their journey homeward, but Robert stood still. "Get up, mule!" he called and laid the switch across his fat flanks. Robert only moved his ears back and would not budge. Bessie got out and tugged at the halter, Big Joe used his switch unsparingly, the boys pushed the wagon from the rear. Robert stood his ground.

"I'll cure him and for all time," said Big Joe,

getting down and collecting twigs and sticks and lighting them in a fire under Robert's belly. The flames leapt higher, Robert's ears shot forward then back. He took a step.

"Look, Pa, it worked," yelled the boys, but too soon. Robert stopped the wagon body directly over the flame. "Come King!" exclaimed Bessie. "Robert trying to burn up our wagon!"

All was confusion, the wagon was on the verge of destruction, suddenly Big Joe grabbed a stick and scattered the fire in all directions and the others followed his example. Then without saying anything he went off down the road to their house and returned with a shovel. He placed a light-wood knot in it, set it a'fire, then held it under Robert's belly. Robert's ears laid back, then he stepped forward and this time Big Joe moved forward also, holding fire close to Robert's skin. Suddenly Robert gave a loud bray, bucked twice, then set off at a terrific pace and did not stop running until he had reached his barn. The family followed on foot. When they finally caught up with him, Bessie said, "That mule sure been visited with Satan this day! He tried to ruin us!"

"Maybe he's got witches in him, Mama," suggested Joseph.

"He do, for sure, she answered, "and I have an idea." She went into the house and returned with a jar of red dirt a friend had sent to her from the hill country. She began to roll it into round red witches' balls to match the ones on their chimney corners. Job and Joseph climbed on Robert's roof and she handed them the balls to place in a row down the center. "Now," said Bessie, satisfied. "This will keep them haunts out of him."

Sure enough, from that day on they never had any trouble with Robert balking. Big Joe claimed it was the fire, Bessie and the boys declared it was red clay balls keeping the witches away.

Bessie led her little family into the house and closed the doors, which were painted Heaven-blue, behind them. She took down her Bible and read aloud until the little boys were nodding and their eyes heavy with sleep. She tucked them between sun-dried sheets and blew out the lamp.

Bessie knelt by her bed and prayed a long, thankful prayer. She thanked the Lord for her man and boys, for their house and land and yard swept

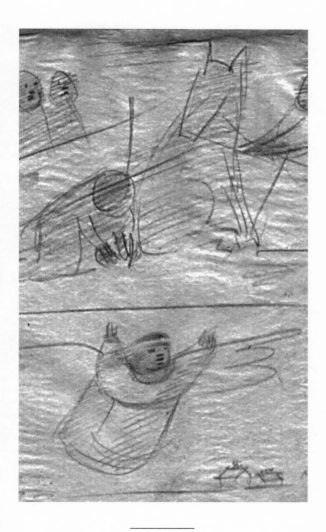

clean of all dropping foliage, and even for Robert. As she prayed a song was given to her. Big Joe fell asleep as she sang it softly to herself.

> *The prayer wheel keeps turnin'*
> *In my heart, in my heart,*
> *The prayer wheel keeps turnin'*
> *In my heart.*
> *I has made my peace alright wid God*
> *As de prayer wheel keeps turnin'*
> *In my heart.*
>
> *I remember when I was in sin*
> *How my sorrows all began*
> *I went down on my knees cryin'*
> *Oh, Lord have mercy, an'*
> *De prayer wheel keeps turnin'*
> *In my heart."*

The words God gave Bessie left her, she bent her head and accepted the long living goodness all about her, then she too fell asleep.

A note on the production of this book

This book was typeset
in 11/15 Weiss with Neuva Bold.

The original illustrations by Jean Charlot
were done in blue and brown pencil on vellum.
A close look may reveal the original manuscript page
placement of some of the drawings.
Over the decades, the vellum has suffered damaged
by moisture and air but the charm
of the drawings has endured. We hope you
will accept them as they were meant to be.